THE WORLD
OF CHAOS

TERRA
CURSE OF THE FOREST

With special thanks to Michael Ford

For Benjamin Grenier

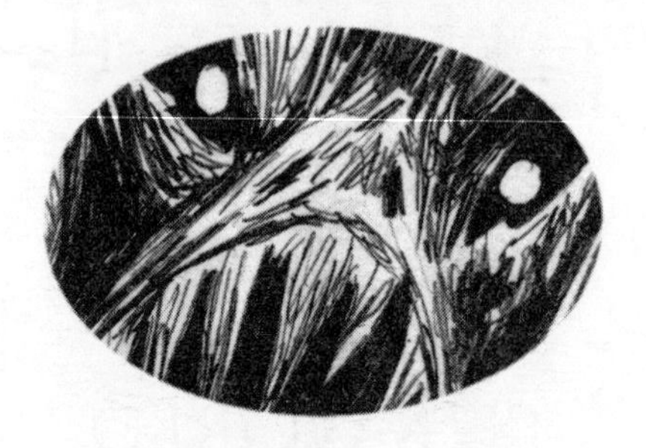

www.beastquest.co.uk

ORCHARD BOOKS
338 Euston Road, London NW1 3BH
Orchard Books Australia
Level 17/207 Kent St, Sydney, NSW 2000

A Paperback Original
First published in Great Britain in 2010

A CIP catalogue record for this book is available from
the British Library.

ISBN 978 1 40830 727 4

8

Printed and bound by CPI Group (UK) Ltd, Croydon, CR0 4YY

The paper and board used in this paperback are natural recyclable
products made from wood grown in sustainable forests. The
manufacturing processes conform to the environmental regulations of
the country of origin.

Orchard Books is a division of Hachette Children's Books,
an Hachette UK company

www.hachette.co.uk

TERRA
CURSE OF THE FOREST

BY ADAM BLADE

ORCHARD

THE ICY D
KAYONIAN MARSHLANDS
KAYONIAN PLAINS
KAYONIAN FOREST

ERT
Kayonia
THE GOLDEN VALLEY
MEATON

Hail, young warriors!

Tom has set out on a Quest of his own choosing, and I have the honour of helping with magic learned from the greatest teacher of them all: my master, Aduro. Tom's challenges will be great: a new kingdom, a lost mother and six more Beasts under Velmal's spell. Tom isn't just fighting to save a kingdom. He's fighting to save those lives closest to him and to prove that love can conquer evil. Can it? Tom will only find out by staying strong and keeping the flame of hope alive. As long as no foul wind blows it out...

Yours truly,

The apprentice, Marc

PROLOGUE

With his axe balanced over his shoulder, Edric picked his way across the forest floor. The crunch of dry leaves beneath his feet sounded deafening; he even imagined he could hear his own heart thumping. Where were the birds in the trees and the animals rustling in the undergrowth?

Light poured down from the gaps between the branches, bathing patches of the forest in Kayonian sunshine. Ferns stirred in the light breeze and fungi ballooned around the tree trunks. This place would be beautiful, if it wasn't so deadly, Edric thought, shivering. Three of his friends had already ventured into the depths of the forest that month. None had returned.

You're mad, he told himself. *You shouldn't have come.*

But Edric had no choice. He wanted to find his friends, and his village needed more wood; the forest was the only place to get it. Without wood they could not fashion any more weapons, and without weapons, how could they ever hope to free themselves from the tyrannical Queen Romaine? Edric still didn't understand why the queen had turned on her people, but she certainly had to be stopped!

He took a swig from his flask and pressed on, watching the shadows warily. He told himself that the stories about the forest weren't true. Nothing lived here except for rabbits and deer.

Certainly no monsters!

Edric caught his foot in something and tripped, crying out as he fell to the mossy ground. It was just a gnarled root. Edric breathed a sigh of relief.

"Stop being silly," he said firmly. Steadying himself against a tree trunk, he rose to his feet. His glance fell on an upturned basket resting on the forest floor. A heap of half-rotton apples lay beside it.

"Gwynneth?" he said. His friend

had gone missing a few days before, but that was definitely her basket.

Edric took a step closer, glancing from side to side. There was no sign of anyone around.

Suddenly, a howl cut through the trees – a strange, high-pitched sound.

"It's just the wind," Edric reassured himself. "Nothing to be scared of."

Leaving the basket behind, he came to a clearing dominated by a tall tree. Its trunk was as straight as an arrow, with no sign of disease or weakness. It would make a perfect battering ram.

Edric planted his feet firmly, hoisted his axe and swung it into the base of the tree. Splinters of bark flew off and the shock of the blow travelled up through his powerful shoulders. He pulled the axe free and swung again.

It wasn't long before the trunk began to totter. One last blow, and with a creak, the wood split. The mighty tree slowly leaned over and Edric scrambled away.

"Timber!" he shouted.

The trunk toppled, slamming into the ground, sending up a cloud of earth and leaves.

Edric set to work, stripping the trunk of its branches. After a while, he straightened up and surveyed his work with pride. He'd need his trusty carthorse to drag the trunk back to his village.

Edric stretched his aching back muscles and mopped the sweat from his forehead.

But what was this?

Another tree, even bigger, stood a few feet away. Vines as thick as

Edric's arm entwined the upper branches. A small white flower sprouted from one of the trailing tendrils.

"How strange that I didn't notice it before," Edric said to himself. "Well, I'm not going to miss this opportunity."

Edric raised his axe, but before he could strike, the bark in the tree split open.

"What...?" From the new gap in the trunk, two yellow eyes glowed, filled with hate.

A rustling from above made Edric look up. Two branches, like arms, snaked down towards him. One wrapped round his waist and the other round his ankle.

"Help!" Edric screamed. "The tree... It's alive!"

He raised his axe to defend himself,

but another branch entwined it and tore it from his grip.

Edric stared in terror at the two eyes. Beneath them, another split appeared. Teeth of black splinters lined the creature's mouth, and the stench of rotting vegetation blasted over Edric's face.

The tree-beast let out a howl of anger, and the ground shook as its roots broke free, dragging clumps of wet earth with them. Edric struggled in the branches, but vines and tendrils descended, coiling around his arms and legs, trapping him. He felt himself being lowered, then dragged towards the churned up earth where the trunk had uprooted itself. Edric dug his heels into the ground, but it was hopeless; the Beast was too strong.

Edric felt his legs being forced into the loose earth. He looked down in terror as bark began to stiffen round his ankles. He couldn't even see his legs anymore – they were encased with leaves and vines. The tendrils climbed higher, wrapping around his chest, then reaching for his neck. As they covered his mouth like a hand,

Edric found he couldn't breathe.

He was trapped inside the tree! The Beast roared in triumph, and Edric wished he'd never ventured into the forest at all.

CHAPTER ONE

A VISITOR AT NIGHT

Tom guided Storm carefully to the edge of the rainbow swamp and onto solid ground.

"Good work," he said, patting his stallion's neck. Storm's legs were coated in sticky mud, and he shook his mane. Silver followed, dragging his paws out of the soggy ground. His fur was flecked with dirt but, happy to be on dry land, he ran in excited circles, barking with delight.

"I'm glad to be out of *that*!" said Elenna.

"Now we've defeated Murk the swamp man," said Tom, "we're one step closer to healing Freya.' He tapped Storm's saddlebag, where the latest ingredient – a linked chain of weeds – was safely stored.

The air suddenly darkened and cooled. Tom shivered. He'd been in Kayonia long enough now to realise the cause. The sun was sinking and the day would soon be over. Silver whined.

"We'll have to find somewhere to camp," said Tom.

Elenna nodded. "We need to rest, anyway," she said. She pointed to some raised ground, where an outcrop of rocks was silhouetted against the horizon. "Up there looks good."

Tom nudged Storm's flanks and they galloped up the incline, scattering loose rocks. The last of the light faded as they reached them. Tom slid off his saddle and began unpacking his stallion's bags. He laid two blankets on the ground, then pulled out some stale bread. Breaking it in half, he offered a piece to Elenna.

"It's all the food we have left," he said.

"Don't worry," Elenna told him, tearing into the bread. "We'll pass a settlement soon and barter for more."

Storm was happy enough. After Tom relieved him of his saddle he found a patch of grass to eat. Silver streaked away to hunt.

"Maybe he'll catch a rabbit or two for us," Elenna laughed.

Tom lit a fire with the last of their wood. They huddled close and warmed their hands. In Kayonia, there was no telling how long the night might last. Sometimes it was over before the fire even got going; other times the darkness lasted long after the embers had died.

As Tom lay down, Kayonia's three moons rose into the sky.

I wonder if my mother can see them, too, he thought, rolling over. Thinking about his mother made him clench his fists in anger. The evil wizard Velmal had cast his poisonous dark magic over her, and plagued Tom with visions. The last time he'd seen Freya, she was weak, and her skin was pale and cracked.

But where was she now? And what torture was Velmal putting her through? They were over halfway through the Quest, but he still needed to find the remaining two ingredients for the potion that would heal her.

"I won't fail you," he whispered.

Suddenly there was a hiss. The fire flared brightly, spraying sparks. Tom sprang away as flames climbed in a spinning spiral. Storm whinnied nervously.

"What is it?" said Elenna.

A shape appeared – first a tall hat, then a body, and finally a pair of boots. The fire died away and standing before them was Marc, Aduro's wizard apprentice.

"You certainly know how to make an entrance," Tom said, laughing as he sat down again.

Marc brushed a cinder from his robes.

"Greetings," he said. "Do you have something for me?"

Tom retrieved Murk's weed chain from Storm's saddlebag. As he handed it to Marc, he saw the wizard's face was lined with worry.

"What is it?" asked Tom.

Marc looked at him with weary eyes and said, "I fear that time is against you." Tom's heart quickened. "War will soon befall Kayonia."

"But we're winning," said Elenna. "We've already defeated four Beasts."

The young wizard shook his head gravely. "I come from Queen Romaine's palace. The kingdom is in turmoil."

He waved his hand and a vision shimmered in the air above them. Fires leapt from buildings, people ran screaming and the clash of metal rang out as a burly man swung his sword against his neighbour. Silver arrived at Elenna's side, growling at the image.

"The people are turning on each other," Tom murmured, horror plunging through him. The vision vanished, leaving a wisp of smoke.

"This is Velmal's doing, isn't it?" Tom said.

"It is," replied Marc. "He turns Kayonians against one another. He causes their crops to fail and anger to spread over the land like a plague. And the people blame the queen."

"What can we do?" asked Tom. "We still need to conquer the two remaining Beasts."

Suddenly there was a sound like a distant trumpet and Marc looked over his shoulder.

"The queen's bugles are sounding," he said. "She calls for her forces to muster. I must leave you."

As Marc's body began to fade, Tom reached out.

"Wait!" he said. "Tell us what to do."

"There is only one thing," said Marc. "You must hurry."

His words blended into the whistle of the breeze through the rocks. Then he was gone.

Tom looked desperately at Elenna. If the queen sent her forces against Velmal, then Freya would be in harm's way. There was no way she could protect herself.

"We need to leave," he said. "Now."

CHAPTER TWO

THE BRINK OF WAR

"But it's still dark," said Elenna. "We won't be able to see the path."

Tom heaved Storm's saddle over the stallion's back and tightened the girth.

"I won't wait here for my mother to die," he said as he mounted Storm. "If we take it slowly, at least we'll cover some distance before dawn."

"You're right," Elenna admitted, climbing up beside him.

With Silver panting beside them, they headed away from the rocky outcrop at a trot. Storm's hooves skidded on the path, but he managed to keep his balance.

Tom had forgotten his tiredness in the rush of determination, but as the moons wheeled away and the sun rose, he blinked wearily in the dazzling daylight. *We haven't slept properly for days,* he thought.

"Something's the matter with Storm," Elenna pointed out.

Tom brought Storm to a halt and stroked his neck. Storm's left front hoof was raised.

"What is it, boy?" he asked, sliding off the saddle. Storm snorted.

Tom crouched down and saw that

Storm's shoe was hanging loose. Guilt flooded through him.

"I'm so selfish," he said. "He must have thrown it on the rocky path. I should never have made us leave under cover of darkness."

He felt a hand on his shoulder. Elenna gave him an understanding smile.

"Don't be hard on yourself," she said. "We all know how you feel about this Quest. Velmal is keeping your mother prisoner."

Silver touched Tom's hand with a wet nose. The show of affection made Tom more determined than ever. "Come on," he said. "We need to find a blacksmith."

He pulled out his magical amulet, turned it over and watched the surface shift into a new map. Lines like silver thread scorched paths crossing the landscape. One glowed brighter than the rest, and led into a dark forest. At the end of the path was the image of a single white flower with seven petals. "That's where we need to go," said Tom. "The flower must be the ingredient."

"But where's the Beast that guards it?" asked Elenna.

Tom peered closer at the amulet: a name appeared dimly: Terra. But then it faded away again.

"Maybe the amulet's magic is broken," said Elenna.

"Or maybe Terra's hiding," Tom said.

Elenna pointed at another part of the map, a short ride from the forest. Little cottages were clustered around a square. Surrounding these were fields filled with grapevines and dotted with copses of trees. "That looks like a village," she said. "And it's almost on the way."

Tom held Storm's reins. "We'll get you fixed up soon," he said to his stallion. "It's the least we can do to thank you."

Tom was expecting rolling pastures of grapevines, laden with fruit, but they didn't appear. The first sign that people lived close by were tree stumps – there were hundreds of them, all bearing axe marks where they'd been hacked down.

"These people must build a lot of houses," said Elenna.

The grapevines in the fields were untended. Most had fallen over, or were dying under their own weight.

Weeds had crawled over the plants and the fruit was rotting.

What happened here? Tom wondered.

He gasped as they crested a small hill. The trees ahead had been cut down as far as the eye could see, all apart from one circular patch of dense, chaotic forest. Checking the amulet, he saw the path ended in the forest.

"That must be where the flower is," he said.

The sound of clanging reached their ears, and clouds of black smoke rose up from below. Tom could see a small village. Leading Storm slowly, he saw that the village was nothing like Errinel. Here, buildings were blackened with soot and window shutters were closed to keep out the ash floating in the air. The sound of mallets and saws joined those of the ringing blacksmith's hammer.

The first person Tom saw was a young woman – she was tying an arrowhead to a wooden shaft. Beside her, a boy was fashioning clubs from pieces of a smashed up chair.

"It's like the whole village has been turned into an armoury!" said Elenna.

An old man nailing hide to a shield eyed them suspiciously as they passed. Tom realised the shield was part of a door torn from its hinges.

They reached the cobbled square at the town centre. Storm was limping badly now. Two huge wheeled catapults stood in front of a blacksmith's shop.

"That place looks as good as any," said Tom. With Elenna beside him, he stooped under the low doorway.

Inside was a girl, not much older than him. She was wearing a thick apron and was leaning over an anvil, hammering sparks off a molten blade.

She looked Tom up and down, and spoke without stopping her work.

"You've got weapons already. So what d'you want?"

Tom was taken aback at her gruffness. "I need a new shoe for my horse," he explained.

The girl snorted. She plunged the hissing metal into a trough of water.

"Well, you won't get one here," she said. "My father will throw a fit if I stop rebellion work."

So that's what's going on! Tom thought.

Elenna stepped forward. "But what are you all rebelling against?"

The girl pulled the sword from the water and inspected the blade. Then she looked at them as though they were stupid. "Where have you been?" she said. "We're rebelling against Queen Romaine, of course!"

Tom shared a look with Elenna. Marc's vision was coming true: the people were preparing for a civil war.

CHAPTER THREE

ENEMIES OF KAYONIA

"War isn't inevitable," urged Tom. "The problems in Kayonia aren't caused by the queen. You have to believe me."

"I wish I could," said the girl. Suddenly she looked much younger. She tossed the sword blade aside. "I remember when we had no need for weapons at all. This village concentrated on its fruit crops – the best in Kayonia…" Tears welled in her eyes.

Tom was about to comfort her, when he heard Storm neigh in alarm. He rushed outside, followed by Elenna and the girl. A plump man was standing beside Tom's stallion, inspecting the horse's strong legs and firm flanks.

"He'd make a fine charger in battle, wouldn't he?" said the man to Tom. "How much do you want for him?"

"He's *not* for sale," said Tom firmly. As the man walked off grumbling, the girl spoke up.

"My name's Rose," she said.

Tom introduced himself and Elenna. "I can't explain now," he told Rose. "But you must listen. Peace is still possible. We're trying to stop the war, and we need our horse to be able to walk properly. If you help us, then perhaps your village will return to normal one day."

"Yes," she said. "I'll do as you ask, but we'll have to be quick." She shot an anxious glance around. "My father's gone to speak with the village elders. If he sees me slacking, he'll beat me."

In the yard, Rose worked to prise off Storm's old shoe. Another horse was standing by – an old carthorse with long hair and sad eyes. "Don't mind Lugger, he's just old," said Rose.

Tom noticed that part of the stable roof was missing, and the timbers were stacked against a wall. Elenna must have noticed too.

"Why are you taking the buildings to pieces?" she asked. "There's a whole forest further along the track."

Rose dropped the old shoe and looked at her with wide eyes. "Oh no," she said. "We couldn't do that." The fear in her voice was unmistakeable.

"Why not?" said Tom. "Isn't the wood good enough?"

Storm remained steady as Rose held a new shoe in place.

"The wood's the best there is," she said. "But it's...well, it's not safe."

Rose hammered nervously at the new shoe without looking up.

She's hiding something, thought Tom. *Is it something to do with Terra?*

"Is there...something in the forest you're afraid of?" he asked.

Rose finished with the horseshoe, and shivered. "The forest has been cursed," she said. "None who go in ever emerge again. We've lost four villagers to the Dark Wood. One of them was Edric." Her eyes welled up. "My brother."

Tom saw Elenna raise her eyebrows. This sounded like the work of a Beast.

Storm tested the new shoe on the cobbles and tossed his mane in gratitude. "As good as new," said Tom. "Thank you for helping us."

A burst of angry shouting erupted from nearby. "Order! Order!" a man cried.

Rose's eyes opened wide in fear. "That's my father! He must be back from seeing the elders in the neighbouring village."

With Silver padding beside them, Tom and Elenna passed through a gate that joined the yard to the main square. Storm accompanied them, and Rose followed. A crowd had gathered since they'd entered the blacksmiths – some were carrying weapons, either makeshift or well-crafted. Tom saw a sickle being waved in the air by a young farmer. On an upturned crate, a man with bulky arms and a thick neck that seemed to disappear into his shoulders was addressing the gathering. *That must be Rose's father,* Tom thought.

"We can't discuss the matter with everyone shouting." he bellowed. "Silence!"

One by one, the people stopped talking, but a woman near the front called in a shrill voice, "We must attack before the queen has a chance to reinforce. I say we march on the capital now. We can pick up more support from surrounding villages."

Her words brought another volley of protests and encouragement. Tom realised the villagers were afraid, as well as angry.

"Are you mad?" said an old man. "Romaine has powerful magic – she must be a witch!"

"He's right," said another. "How else can you explain the disappearances in the forest?"

Elenna squeezed Tom's arm. "If only we could tell them the real cause," she whispered.

Tom shook his head. "They wouldn't believe us," he replied.

"That's him!" said a voice. Suddenly the crowd turned towards Tom. The tubby man who'd been looking at Storm was pointing at him. "That's the lad who thinks his horse is too good to go into battle." Boos and hisses spread through the crowd. "He has a shield too!" said his accuser. "And a sword."

The people began to advance, pressing Tom and Elenna back against the wall of the blacksmiths.

"You don't understand," said Tom.

He kept his hand off his sword; he didn't want to make this situation any worse. Silver growled and snapped his teeth.

"Her bow and arrows look decent, as well," said the plump man.

"We're here to help," said Elenna. Tom noticed that she had also left her bow slung across her shoulder. "Queen Romaine is not your enemy."

Her words only seemed to inflame the crowd further. "You dare to defend her?" said the massive blacksmith. "Well, then, you can be only one thing: spies!"

"Kill them!" shouted the man with the sickle. "Kill the spies!"

CHAPTER FOUR

THE FROZEN FOREST

Several of the approaching villagers had levelled their weapons. Tom saw a pike, its sharp blade catching the sun. The look in the eyes of the woman holding it was even sharper. A man with a desperate expression was lifting a double-headed axe. Judging by his thick forearms, Tom guessed he was used to chopping down trees with ease.

Rose leapt in front of them and held out her hands.

"They're not spies," she cried. "They're good people."

Her father stepped forward and seized her roughly by the arm. "That's enough, my girl. Leave this to your elders." He stared hard at Tom and Elenna. "Kill them both."

The man with the axe rushed forward, swinging his weapon.

"Mount Storm!" Tom shouted to Elenna as he ran to meet his attacker. He ducked and the axe whistled over his head. He kicked the man in the back of the legs to topple him over. Elenna had mounted Storm and was spurring him forward. The crowd backed away as the stallion reared, wheeling his hooves.

Silver snapped at a man with a mallet, then leapt up onto a wall and ran across a low thatched roof. Tom could see that he was safe.

"Climb up," shouted Elenna.

Tom took a blow to his shield as he leapfrogged into the saddle behind his friend. Someone grabbed his foot, but he kicked them away.

"Get us out of here!" Tom yelled. Storm charged at the heaving mass of villagers. With shouts of terror, they parted and the stallion careered across the square.

"After the spies!" came a cry. "Don't let them escape!"

Silver appeared, leaping gracefully over a water trough. "Good boy!" Elenna called.

His friend steered Storm onto the road out of the village. Tom risked a look behind. Men were mounting horses to give chase. Rose was still struggling in her father's grasp. She managed to raise a hand and called out, "Good luck!"

We'll need it! Tom thought.

They passed between simple huts and derelict farming equipment. Behind them, hooves pounded the ground. The villagers weren't giving up easily! Tom saw a wiry man clutching a spear leading the pack.

"Quicker!" he urged, and Elenna dug her heels harder into Storm's side. Tom gripped Elenna's waist with one hand and fumbled to pull his amulet out with the other. He saw that they were on the wrong path, heading away from the forest.

"Take a left at the crossroads," he shouted over the thundering hooves.

Elenna steered Storm around the corner, churning up mud. A rallying cry went up behind, and their pursuers changed their course as well. But when Tom saw what was ahead, his heart fell.

A gate, as tall as two men, tied with thick twine. It was set into a wall that was far too high for Storm to jump.

We're trapped!

Elenna must have seen it too. She looked over her shoulder. "Take the reins!"

Tom fumbled for the leather straps. As he held on, keeping Storm galloping steadily at the gates, Elenna unhooked her bow and strung an arrow. She aimed at the gates. Even with the movement of Storm's gait, her hands were steady.

The gates were twenty paces away, and behind them their enemies were closing in. She'd only get one shot.

Elenna released the arrow, which fizzed through the air and sliced the binding on the gate.

"You did it!" Tom whooped.

Elenna took back the reins and with a burst of speed, Storm pushed through the gate and raced on, with Silver following, barking in delight. Now they were in open country. Ahead loomed the Dark Forest, stranded like an island in the midst of the flat plain.

Still the villagers didn't give up the chase, but Tom's stallion – the best racer in Avantia – had the advantage. Gradually they pulled away. In front of them loomed the forest. Tom saw the chasing Kayonians suddenly wheel their horses around.

"Stop!" he said to Elenna. As Storm slowed, his flanks slick with sweat, Tom pointed behind them. The wiry rider had raised his spear to halt the other villagers.

"Why have they stopped?" asked Elenna, breathing heavily.

Tom looked toward the forest. "They're scared," he said. "Remember what Rose said. They think this place is cursed."

"Then let's take it slowly," said Elenna. As Storm trotted on, Silver stayed close. Tom checked the amulet again.

"Funny," he said. "The white flower has moved."

It was still in the forest, but now the amulet showed its position at the furthermost edge.

"What sort of flower moves?" asked Elenna.

A chill passed over Tom's body. Where Beasts and evil magic were concerned, he'd learned to expect the unexpected.

But as Storm carried them into the forest, his fear all but vanished.

"It's beautiful!" gasped Elenna.

The trees were straight and tall, with a lush canopy of bright green leaves that filtered the sunlight into peaceful glades. The air smelled as fresh as the Avantian Plains.

Suddenly Storm halted.

"What is it, boy?" asked Elenna, lightly nudging his sides.

But Storm didn't budge. He gave a panicked whinny.

"Something's spooked him," said Tom, sliding from the saddle to stroke his stallion's nose. Storm's eyes were wide. "Come on, boy! We've got a Beast to face."

Tom took the bridle and gave a gentle tug, but Storm tossed his head and dug in his heels. On the ground beside him, Silver whined and sat back on his haunches. The hair on the scruff of his neck was standing straight as he stared between the trees.

"Tom!" hissed Elenna. "Look!"

A spindly-legged deer was standing still as a statue beside a tree, almost camouflaged against its bark. Tom was surprised he hadn't spotted it before.

He stepped closer, but the creature didn't stir. Only when Tom was a few paces away did he understand. It was a *statue*! Each of its hairs seemed to be carved from wood. But something wasn't right.

The finest carpenter in the land couldn't make something so realistic, Tom thought.

He looked around. Nearby, on the low branch of a tree, an owl was perched. It, too, was motionless, its feathers stiff. And below, a wooden fox lurked, its tail curled in the air.

"Something did this to them," Tom whispered. "Something terrible."

CHAPTER FIVE

A HORRIBLE DISCOVERY

Elenna shivered and crouched beside Silver, ruffling his fur. She didn't take her eyes from the motionless deer. Tom walked up and touched its neck. Solid wood.

"Perhaps that's what happened to the poor villagers, too," she said. "Like Rose's brother. Perhaps that's what will happen to us!"

Tom gripped his sword hilt tightly. Velmal's evil knew no bounds.

"I'm willing to take my chances. I can't expect you to do the same, though. This is my Quest, after all."

Elenna looked at him with steel in her eyes.

"It's my Quest, too," she said. "I won't back down."

Tom smiled at his companion. "We'd better leave Silver and Storm out of harm's way," he said. "It's just you and me this time."

They led their animal companions back to the edge of the forest. Thankfully, the villagers seemed to have given up the chase and were nowhere to be seen.

They don't think we'll make it out alive, thought Tom grimly.

"We'll see you soon," Tom told

Storm and Silver. The wolf sat alert by the stallion's legs.

With Elenna at his side and the amulet in his palm, Tom led the way among the trees. He hadn't noticed it before, but the forest was silent apart from the sounds of their cushioned footsteps. No birds were twittering in the trees, no rabbits were scuttling across the ground.

Quiet as a grave.

The air felt colder as the trees grew more densely together, with less light penetrating the thick branches above. Elenna gripped his arm and pointed. Ahead was a twisted tree with folds of bark like a hanging curtain. But Elenna was looking at what lay on the ground at its roots: a hunting knife, with a rusty blade.

The villagers had been here…

Then Tom spotted an axe, half buried in fallen leaves. Lying across the forest floor was a huge tree, very straight. Branches had been chopped away from the trunk, leaving it ready to be transported back to the village.

Perhaps this is where Edric met his end, Tom thought.

He walked over and picked up the knife and the axe. "Extra weapons might come in useful," he explained, passing the hunting knife to Elenna.

To fix his bearings, he checked the amulet. The flower had moved again. Not as far as last time, but it had definitely moved. He showed it to Elenna.

"How can we catch a moving target?" she hissed in frustration.

She was right, but Tom forced himself not to give up hope. His mother's life was in his hands; if he gave up now... Tom shook himself; he didn't want to think of the consequences if he failed in his Quest.

They continued, passing a group of wooden rabbits, silently alert with pointed ears. All these bewitched animals, but not a single human being. Where was Rose's brother, and the other lost villagers?

A light breeze rustled the branches above, and some of the trees seemed to groan softly. Tom swallowed.

It's just the wind, he told himself.

Soon they reached a twisted tree. Elenna looked at it closely, her forehead creasing into a frown.

"Isn't that the same tree we passed earlier?" she said. "The one where the knife was?"

Tom peered closely at the folds in

the trunk, exactly like a draped curtain. "It must be."

"Then we are lost," said Elenna, her eyes wide.

But Tom had been carefully following the route traced on the amulet. They'd been travelling in a straight line.

"There is another possibility," he said. "The trees are *moving*."

As the words left his mouth, the forest was plunged into darkness.

Elenna groaned. "Night again! What now?"

Tom waited for his eyes to adjust. The trees were like spectres standing guard around them. Tom almost imagined he was being watched.

It's my mind playing tricks, that's all.

"We'll make camp," he said decisively. "And light a fire. If we

can't find the Beast, maybe the flames will bring it to us."

"There's plenty of wood around," said Elenna.

Tom shouldered the axe and headed to the nearest tree, a small one not much taller than he was.

This shouldn't take long, he thought.

He raised the axe, ready to swing, when a terrible sound shrieked into the night. Tom stumbled backwards and dropped the axe.

"What was that?" Elenna said, running up beside him.

Tom stood up and glanced around. "I don't know. A bird, perhaps?"

"I've never heard a bird like that," she said, her voice quaking. "It sounded so...*desperate*."

A rustling sound made him look back towards the tree. In the moonlight, Tom could see that its leaves were shaking.

"That's odd," he said. "I can't feel any breeze."

He stepped closer to the tree and ran his hand along the branch. It felt strangely warm to his touch. At the end of the branch, it split into five thinner branches.

Almost like fingers.

Realisation crept up Tom's spine. He looked down. Near the ground the trunk was warped, and seemed to separate into two roots.

It can't be.

"Elenna..." he murmured."I think..."

"What?" she asked.

There was no denying it. It narrowed near the top of the trunk, then widened again. Beneath a crown of moss the trunk had two indentations, side by side, and a bump beneath.

Eyes. A nose... It was a head!

"Elenna," Tom said slowly. "There's a person inside!"

CHAPTER SIX

TERRA!

Elenna's hand flew to her mouth, then she pointed at the surrounding trees, one by one. Dotted among the taller trunks were several smaller trees, all with the same distinctive shape silhouetted against the three moons.

"I think those trees have people in them, too," she gasped.

So this is where the villagers ended up!

Tom let the axe fall to the ground and stepped closer to the tree.

"Can you hear me?" he asked.

No voice replied, but the leaves rustled.

"Whoever it is can't talk," he said. "But perhaps we can free them."

Tom unsheathed his sword and placed the blade against the bark. With a careful sawing motion, he scraped it back.

The tree screeched like a vulture and the sound carried across the forest.

"Tom, stop!" said Elenna. "You're hurting it."

All around, the other trees took up the agonised cry. Tom dropped his sword and placed his hands over his ears. Dark sap oozed from the gash in the bark, pooling in the tree's roots.

Tom couldn't make out the colour in the gloom, but he had a horrible fear that it was red. Just like blood. Slowly, the wailing died down, to be replaced with a low moaning. The trees seemed to be talking over each other. But what were they saying?

Tom strained his ears as the chorus came into unison. They were repeating a single word.

"It sounds like, 'terror, terror, terror'," said Elenna. "They must be afraid."

In the distance, Silver added his howl to the awful chanting.

Tom hurriedly pulled out the amulet and read the Beast's name again. Fear took his heart in its icy fingers.

"Terra!" he muttered. "Elenna, it's the name of the Beast. It must be coming."

The chanting rose to a crescendo, then suddenly died away. Tom shouted into the eerie silence. "I don't know if you understand me," he called. "But while there's blood in my veins, I will defeat the Beast that did this to you!"

Dawn came quickly, the bright light forcing Tom awake. He and Elenna had reluctantly settled down for the night; there was nothing they could do whilst the forest was plunged in darkness. Tom squinted in the sudden daylight. He sat up and shook Elenna. His friend awoke, pushing her hair out of her face and rubbing her eyes. Her brow creased in confusion as she paced over to a nearby tree.

"Tom," she said, running her hand over the bark. "Was this tree here last night?"

He sensed danger in the air. "I don't think so." The thought of the trees shifting in the darkness made him feel uneasy.

He looked closely at the new tree. It was the biggest he'd seen in the forest. The trunk was so wide it would have taken five men to loop their arms around its girth. But if it hadn't been for its size, Tom would have guessed the tree was diseased. The bark was rough and cracked with age. Patches of green fungus grew over the surface and the smell that twitched his nostrils was rotten. Looking further up, the branches were entwined in coils of vines like strangling snakes. And among them sprouted a tiny white flower.

"Elenna," he said in excitement. "The magic ingredient – I can see it!"

His friend came to his side and grinned. "Well, that was easy. Why don't you climb up and get it? With any luck we won't even have to face a Beast on this Quest!"

Tom looked warily about. He certainly couldn't *see* any danger.

"You keep watch," he said.

Elenna put an arrow to her bow, and nodded. "Be careful."

Tom had climbed hundreds of trees near his village in Avantia. He walked to the foot of the tree and scrambled up the first part with ease, ignoring the horrible smell. There were plenty of cracks to use as handholds.

With his foot lodged in a split, he reached for a low branch. Just as his fingers were closing around it, the branch creaked and lifted away. Tom lost his footing and plummeted to the ground, jarring his ankle. Elenna screamed.

Tom looked up and saw the branch snaking towards her. It wrapped quickly around her waist and snatched her off her feet.

"No!" Tom yelled, jumping up and running towards her with his sword drawn. He swung the blade at the branch, but he missed. Before he could attack again, another branch descended and clubbed him so hard in the chest that he flew backwards.

His sword arced into the air and landed several paces away. As he tried to stand, his ankle was seized by one of the tree's massive roots. He tugged and tugged but couldn't free himself. In the tree trunk, two eyes appeared between splits of the bark, yellow and deadly. Beneath them was a slash like an axe-cut. It twisted into an evil smile.

So this was Terra, the curse of the forest!

CHAPTER SEVEN

BURIED ALIVE

Elenna cried out again and Tom saw her being spun round in a blur. Earth scattered from her feet as the Beast drove her into the ground.

He's planting her! Tom realised.

Again he clawed at the root that held him, but without a weapon it was useless. When she was buried to her knees, Elenna's body went limp. For a moment, Tom feared the worst.

Could his friend be dead?

No, her eyelids fluttered, but her skin was as pale as snow.

The tree-beast cackled. The white flower in the upper branches seemed to pulsate, its glowing petals throbbing with life.

Just like a heart.

Tom looked from Elenna's weakened form back to the flower.

It's sucking her life-force. he thought. "Hold on!" he called to his friend.

He writhed against the root desperately. Elenna would never end up like the other villagers, not if he could help it. But with his sinews stretched almost to breaking point, he fell back, dripping with sweat. Elenna was buried even deeper, to her waist.

A movement caught his eye.

Beyond Elenna, the tree-person he'd hurt was swaying. One of its arm-branches seemed to bend under a great weight, and a soft moaning filled the forest.

With what must have been an almighty effort, the twigs that formed its fingers stretched for something on the ground. Tom saw it was holding the axe he'd dropped. The small tree hurled it through the air; Tom caught the spinning handle.

"Thank you!" he called out, then set to work chopping the root that held him. As the blade bit, Terra bellowed with fury and the forest floor shook like an earthquake. The Beast lifted its foot, releasing Tom's ankle. He rolled aside as a massive branch hit the ground to crush him.

Tom swiftly leapt over another branch that tried to sweep his legs from under him, and darted away. Thank goodness for Tagus' horseshoe, which gave him speed. If Tom had moved any slower, he'd have been knocked to the ground. He finally reached Elenna. He swung his axe at the branch wrapped around her.

Terra roared in fury and uncoiled his arm. Tom swung again, but the Beast crashed off among the other trees, trailing its soil-clad roots. For such a giant creature, Terra moved quickly.

Elenna sagged to the ground. Tom caught her with one hand and used his shield to scoop away the soil around her legs as she mumbled softly. When she was free, Tom carried her to a nearby tree stump. She was weak, and Tom realised with a shudder that if he'd left it any longer she might not have made it.

Tom unhooked his flask and helped her take a sip. "Take it easy," he said. "You've been through a lot."

She drank a gulp and spluttered. The colour returned to her cheeks

"I was being buried alive," she said. "I couldn't move."

When she could support herself, Tom left her for a moment and went to the tree that had saved him. There was no sign of Terra, though in a forest full of trees, the Beast could conceal itself anywhere.

Tom was pleased that the bark seemed to have healed from where he'd scraped it the day before. But the branches drooped, as though the person inside was weaker than ever.

"Thank you," Tom said. "You saved our lives."

The leaves rustled a little. The person was alive, but only just. Tom hoped he could defeat the Beast and free them before it was too late.

Returning to Elenna's side, he helped her to her feet.

"How can we possibly get the flower?" she said. "It's so high up, and Terra can run away and hide whenever he chooses."

Tom thought hard for a moment, then pulled out the amulet. "The Beast will come to us, I know it will. It just needs time to recover. We need to make sure we're ready. If we can lay some sort of trap, perhaps we can climb up and get the ingredient."

He knew it wasn't much of a plan. How could they stop a murdering tree Beast? *But it's the only plan we have,* he thought. "Are you up to it?" he asked Elenna.

She hoisted her quiver over her shoulder and looked around. "I'm always ready to face another Beast."

Tom picked up his sword and sheathed it.

"We'll find you soon, Terra!" he shouted.

CHAPTER EIGHT

A TRAP

Tom took out his amulet. The white flower was being carried in a wide arc around the edge of the forest. Occasionally, Terra's pained and angry howls filled the air.

"It won't be long before he's back," said Elenna. "Perhaps if we dig a hole, Terra might fall in?"

Tom shook his head. "Terra knows this forest better than anyone – he won't be fooled. Plus, we could never dig a hole deep enough. There must be another way..."

His eyes fell on the tree that had been chopped down and abandoned. A plan quickly formed in Tom's mind. He pointed at the half-finished battering ram.

"We could use that!" he said.

Elenna's forehead wrinkled in confusion. "I don't understand," she said. "What good is a tree trunk?"

Tom was already gathering up the vines that littered the forest floor. He stretched one between his hands and pulled it to show how strong it was. "We use these to hoist the battering ram up into the trees. Then, when Terra comes this way again, we let it swing back. With any luck it will knock him over."

A smile came slowly to Elenna's lips. "It might work, I suppose..."

"It'll have to work," said Tom. "Come on, help me tie the vines into ropes."

Together they cut the thickest vines into lengths and then knotted them together. It was hard work, and Tom regularly checked the amulet to make sure Terra wasn't sneaking up on them. He couldn't help thinking about his mother. Where was Freya, and was she still alive? Tom knew there was no time to waste.

When the ropes were fashioned, Elenna fastened an arrow to each end, and loosed it over the branches above. They tied the other ends around the huge fallen trunk.

"It looks heavy," said Tom. "I'll need your help."

Side by side, they each grabbed a vine rope and began hoisting the massive log high into the tree. It was backbreaking work, and Tom grunted as he took the strain. With sweat pouring from his brow, he lifted the battering ram a fraction at a time.

"Keep pulling!" Tom grimaced. "We're nearly there."

The rope burned his palms and his arms felt like they'd be pulled from their sockets, but he didn't give up. The image of his mother's pale face drove him on.

"You won't win, Velmal," he said under his breath.

When the log was hanging thirty feet up, hidden among the leaves, Tom and Elenna tied the ends of the rope off around a tree root. The battering ram swung gently above.

"What now?" said Elenna, breathing heavily.

"We wait," said Tom.

He wasn't sure how much time passed. It could have been mere moments, or it could have been half a Kayonian day. There was no way of measuring time in this strange new world.

A thundering sound reached their ears. The ground vibrated and the leaves on the trees began to shake.

The sound of splintering wood grew louder. Terra came into the clearing, scuttling on roots that churned up small clumps of earth. He stood over the bark-encased Kayonians with his yellow eyes narrowed. The Beast opened his jagged mouth, blasting foul air over Tom and Elenna. Then, resting on his sturdy, mould-caked roots, he walked towards them, creaking and snapping his claw-like branches.

Elenna dived for cover behind a tree. In the time it took Tom to take a breath she placed two arrows to her bow and loosed them. Terra jerked to the side, and one shaft sailed harmlessly through his leaves. The second lodged above his eye.

The Beast paused and thrashed with pain, emitting a deafening screech.

"Good shot!" cried Tom.

Terra reached out with a branch and closed his wooden claws over the arrow. With a tug he pulled it free and threw it to the ground. His glowing eyes were on Elenna and he lumbered forwards, reaching with his branches. Elenna ducked behind the tree as the Beast snarled and scraped around her.

Tom wasn't going to let his friend get caught again. He took up the axe, raised it above his head and ran at Terra.

With a war cry, Tom sunk the axe's blade into the Beast's trunk. A huge groan erupted. Tom tried to free the axe blade, but couldn't. As Terra turned, Tom was thrown sideways and rolled across the forest floor. When he stood up, Terra was bearing down on him – he was also right beneath the trap. But where was Elenna?

"Cut the rope!" Tom shouted.

Terra snaked out a branch that whipped round Tom's ankle; before he could do anything, he was flipped upside down, hanging above the ground. The blood rushed to his head.

Tom flailed uselessly as he was pulled closer to Terra's trunk. His vision cleared and he saw the Beast's mouth, gaping with rotting black splinters of wood. His blood went cold as he imagined them puncturing his flesh.

"Elenna!" he shouted again. "Help me!"

The mouth was so close, dripping with sticky black sap…

Tom closed his eyes and waited to die.

CHAPTER NINE

ALL OR NOTHING

There was a snap. Tom looked up to see the battering ram swing in a great arc, thudding into Terra's trunk. The Beast's eyes rolled back.

The branches around Tom's ankle loosened and he fell heavily onto the ground. Elenna was standing, with his sword in her hand, and above Terra the battering ram swung, slowly losing momentum.

Elenna must have cut the rope!

The Beast stumbled dizzily.

"Out of the way!" Tom called. "He's going to fall!"

Terra tipped headlong towards him, his branches limp. Tom leapt clear as the leaves and twigs raked past, scratching his face. He cried out in pain. With a *boom,* Terra's trunk smashed into the ground.

Elenna rushed to Tom and held out his sword. "Quick!" she cried. "Get the flower before he wakes up."

Tom sprang to his feet and picked up his sword. Terra's massive roots were upturned beside him, writhing weakly. Tom leapt onto the trunk and ran along towards the upper branches. The white flower shone against the dark vines.

The Beast was stirring, and the trunk rocked so much that Tom fell forwards. He crawled along, cutting his knees on the bark. Tom ignored the pain; the flower was close.

Suddenly it felt as though the world was tipping over. Terra was righting himself and Tom was lifted into the air. He slid off the trunk and reached with his free hand for a branch. He caught one with his fingertips, but his shield slid off his arm. The Beast bellowed with rage and flexed its limbs, standing tall again. Tom hung from the branch and swallowed as he saw the ground, far below. The flower was tantalisingly close, but he couldn't think about it now.

If I fall from this height, without Arcta's feather, I'll break my back for sure.

Terra's eyes fixed on him. The Beast jerked his branch, shaking Tom from side to side to dislodge him. Tom felt his fingers coming loose.

If only I had the gloves from Rokk, but they're in Storm's saddlebag!

"I can't hold on!" he called to Elenna. She was running back and forth below, ready to catch him. *She hasn't got a chance,* he thought.

Terra roared and thrashed violently.

Tom's grip came free; he cartwheeled through the air and began to plummet. He expected to crunch into the ground, but something soft broke his fall. Tom felt leaves against his skin and realised he was cushioned in the branches of a small tree. But the limbs seemed to move of their own accord; they lowered him to the ground. As his feet found the forest floor, Tom realised that the branches belonged to one of the human trees.

"You saved me!" he gasped.

All around the clearing, the smaller trees were rustling their branches. Some were even heaving their roots clear of the soil.

They want to help me defeat Terra!

The *whizz* of an arrow startled Tom. Terra was pursuing Elenna. Every few steps she turned and released an arrow. Several shafts were lodged in the Beast's trunk, but they only seemed to enrage him more. Tom saw that Elenna's quiver was almost empty. He had to think quickly.

Tom's eyes fell upon the vine hanging where Elenna had cut it; he realised what he could do. "Elenna!" he shouted, beckoning her over. "Come this way."

His friend loosed her last arrow at Terra and changed direction. Tom snatched up the vine and sprinted around one of the trees that had caught him. "I need you to stand firm," he said, wrapping the rope twice around the tree's roots. Elenna was getting close, with Terra looming over her. Tom darted back to the big tree and coiled the rope around the base of its trunk. The vine stretched taut, a foot above the ground. Elenna saw it and vaulted over the top.

Terra charged, one lumbering step at a time. *Come on!* Tom urged. *Just a little further.*

The Beast lunged after Elenna, reaching with his stiff claws. As he passed over the vine, his roots snagged. For a moment, Tom feared the vine wouldn't hold – but it did! Terra tipped slowly, struggling to free his root-feet, but it was too late. With a mighty roar he fell over, and with the sound of branches splintering, the Beast slammed into the ground.

This time Tom was ready. He drew his sword and leapt up beside the flower. With a single stroke he sliced through the stem.

Terra moaned as his bark began to buckle and crack. His eyes swivelled in mad panic, and his branches squirmed, tearing up the earth. Rot – black and grey – spread over his trunk, eating it away. With a final cry, the trunk collapsed in on itself and sank into the ground.

As soon as the Beast had vanished, the trees around began to shake and squirm. A section of bark fell from the one nearest to Tom, revealing a patch of pale skin beneath. From the end of a branch, fingers pushed through bark and began to claw at the trunk, tearing away larger pieces. A man's head broke out, gasping for air. Slowly, all around, people emerged from the trees and stared at each other, smiling, stretching their arms and legs, and pulling the remaining pieces of foliage away.

Elenna jumped for joy. "We did it!"

One man still had the rope tangled around his feet. He kicked it away and ran up to Tom. He pumped his hand up and down in a handshake.

"You saved us!" he said. "I thought I'd be trapped in there forever. I didn't know who would look after my little sister Rose..."

The noise of pounding hooves made everyone turn. Storm burst into the clearing, with Silver scampering alongside, tongue lolling. Elenna laughed and shook her finger. "We told you two to stay...oh!"

Two deer gambolled past. Then a fox, sniffing the ground, darted through Storm's hooves. The air was filled with birdsong. A brightly coloured bird flittered above, before coming to rest on a branch.

Life was returning to the forest!

CHAPTER TEN

VELMAL'S REVENGE

Rabbits bounced amongst the flowers and nibbled on the remains of Terra's leaves. Already, where the Beast had fallen, hundreds of beautiful white flowers were blossoming. Tom placed his flower carefully in his tunic as the Kayonians greeted each other happily. The woodsman introduced himself as Edric, and the others as

Gwynneth, Simon, and Caitlin.

"You must return with us to the village," said Edric, retrieving his axe.

Elenna looked nervous. "We had to run away from your village. The people there thought we were spies!"

"Well," said Gwynneth, "we'll make sure they don't make the same mistake again."

Tom helped her onto Storm's back, while he and Elenna walked at their side. The air of the forest was fresh again, and sunlight dappled the ground. Somewhere, a woodpecker was knocking against a tree. Silver chased a squirrel joyfully.

Tom led the procession back along the path to the village. When they reached the broken gate, he heard a roar of voices beyond it.

"What's going on?" asked Edric.

Tom headed cautiously towards the main square, and he heard a voice he recognised all too well: Velmal.

"Who do you think caused the grape harvest to fail?" the evil wizard shouted.

"Romaine!" chanted the crowd.

"And why do traders avoid you?"

"Romaine!" was the reply.

"Wait here," said Tom to the others, walking on. He reached the square and saw the villagers gathered together with their backs to him. They were all facing the Dark Wizard, who stood on the back of a cart addressing them, dressed in black. His long hair whipped around his pale face as he spoke.

"And who has killed the innocents in the forest?" Velmal shouted.

"It was the queen!" yelled Rose's

father, the blacksmith.

Tom drew his sword and pointed it at Velmal.

"He's lying to you!" he shouted. The crowd turned, their faces darkening as they saw Tom.

"It's the spy!" said one. They moved towards him.

"Stop!" shouted the woman Tom rescued from Terra.

"Caitlin!" said several people in astonishment. One man stepped out, with tears welling in his eyes. "My wife! Is it really you?"

"This boy and his friend are not your enemies," said the woman. "They saved us all."

The other rescued villagers stepped forward and ran towards the crowd. They hugged in small groups. The square was filled with excited voices.

Edric embraced his father. Tom's heart swelled with pride at the lives saved by his Quest.

"Enough!" boomed Velmal. "We must march on Queen Romaine!"

The villagers fell silent and looked confusedly between Tom and Velmal.

"He's the one you should be fighting," said Tom. "It was his magic that imprisoned your people in the forest. He wants to overturn the queen so he can rule your land."

Velmal's eyes flashed in anger. Rose's father pointed his staff at him. "Leave our village now," he bellowed. "Or face the consequences."

Velmal cackled. "You couldn't harm me, foolish man." With a burst of light, Velmal began to disappear into a swirling, purple smoke cloud. The crowd gasped and fell back. Several people screamed.

Tom gripped his sword. "Leave him to me!" he shouted. He ran at Velmal, vaulting up onto the cart. But as he stabbed, the wizard's body faded into the purple mist.

"Fight me, coward!" Tom called.

"I have bigger things to fight than a mere boy," snarled Velmal. His cloak folded in on itself, and before Tom could speak, he turned into a raven with a deadly sharp beak, and feathers black as pitch. With a ragged *caw*, it circled, then flew north.

After the villagers had settled down, Edric approached Tom.

"We owe you an apology," he said.

Tom smiled. "It's not necessary. Velmal's magic is powerful; it poisons people's minds."

"Still," said Edric. "We'd like you to stay for a feast tonight. We don't have much, but what we have you are welcome to."

Tom shook his head. "Thank you," he said, taking hold of Storm's reins. "But we still have work to do in Kayonia. A Quest that cannot wait."

Edric nodded in understanding. "I wish you good fortune."

Tom mounted Storm, and Elenna climbed up behind him. "Farewell," he said to the assembled villagers.

He guided Storm back out of the village for the second time, but this time to the sound of cheers. They reached open ground. Tom was about to urge his stallion on, when a stabbing pain sliced through his head.

Tom cried out in pain as he slid helplessly from the saddle.

"Tom!" Elenna said. "What's the matter?"

He hit the ground hard, but it was nothing compared with the agony behind his eyes. The pressure was building and he thought his head would explode.

"Talk to me!" said Elenna.

Her voice became distant and Tom could only moan and press his palms against his temples. Blackness descended like a veil.

A vision swam in front of his eyes:

a woman lying limp of the ground. Her face turned towards him and Tom saw it was Freya. Her face was empty of life.

"Mother," he murmured, reaching a hand towards her.

Her cracked and bloodless lips did not move. There was a sound of deep, cruel laughter.

Tom tried to touch his mother's face, but the vision began to shrink away. "Come back!" Tom pleaded.

There were hands on his shoulders and Tom was aware of someone talking.

"Tom?"

He blinked and saw Elenna. He was lying on the ground, just outside the village gates. Storm nudged him gently with his nose, his bridle clanking. "I'm all right," Tom mumbled, standing unsteadily.

"What happened?" asked Elenna.

"Some sort of vision," said Tom. "We have to find the final ingredient. Quickly."

Ignoring the weakness in his legs, he climbed back into the saddle. Elenna gripped his waist.

"What did you see?" asked his friend anxiously.

"The future, I think," he said. "Elenna, we've got to stop it."

Here's a sneak preview of Tom's next exciting adventure!

Meet

VESPICK THE WASP QUEEN

Only Tom can free the Beasts from Velmal's wicked enchantment...

PROLOGUE

Queen Romaine of Kayonia gazed angrily at a wasp that flew through the window of her north turret. She batted it to the floor and crushed it under her heel. The young wizard Marc was speaking to her, but she couldn't hear because of the buzzing in her ears.

"Speak up!" she said.

Marc moved closer to her. "Your Majesty, the plague of wasps is getting worse," he reported. "Your people are beginning to panic. Something must be done."

Letting out a sigh, the queen paced from one side of the turret room to the other. Her copper-coloured hair flicked out behind her and her knuckles were white from gripping her deadly bone staff so tightly.

"The wasps have chased away the last of my palace guards," she said with a growl of frustration. "Those who haven't gone to deal with the rioters and looters. The kingdom has been plunged into utter chaos." She banged her staff on the floor. "I am a warrior queen, but against this threat I am helpless!"

"Your Majesty— " Marc began.

He broke off as the sound of screams from below rose above the buzzing. Queen Romaine rushed to the window of the tower, with the young wizard by her side. Leaning out, she gazed down into the city square.

The wasps had formed themselves into a swirling, writhing swarm. They danced above the ground, clustering around a shape that the queen couldn't make out clearly. Then she caught her breath in a gasp of horror as the cloud of wasps divided into separate swarms.

Hovering above the square was a creature as tall as two large men. Four fluttering wings sprouted from its back. A human-shaped torso ended in a curious furry body striped in yellow and black. It tapered into a long, cruel sting that glowed brilliant green.

"She must be the queen wasp!" Romaine breathed.

Follow this Quest to the end in VESPICK THE WASP QUEEN.

Win an exclusive Beast Quest T-shirt and goody bag!

Tom has battled many fearsome Beasts and we want to know which one is your favourite! Send us a drawing or painting of your favourite Beast and tell us in 30 words why you think it's the best.

Each month we will select **three** winners to receive a Beast Quest T-shirt and goody bag!

Send your entry on a postcard to
BEAST QUEST COMPETITION
Orchard Books, 338 Euston Road, London NW1 3BH.

Australian readers should email:
childrens.books@hachette.com.au

New Zealand readers should write to:
Beast Quest Competition, 4 Whetu Place, Mairangi Bay, Auckland NZ, or email: childrensbooks@hachette.co.nz

Don't forget to include your name and address. Only one entry per child.

Good luck!

Beast Quest®

- ☐1. Ferno the Fire Dragon
- ☐2. Sepron the Sea Serpent
- ☐3. Arcta the Mountain Giant
- ☐4. Tagus the Horse-Man
- ☐5. Nanook the Snow Monster
- ☐6. Epos the Flame Bird

Beast Quest:
The Golden Armour

- ☐7. Zepha the Monster Squid
- ☐8. Claw the Giant Monkey
- ☐9. Soltra the Stone Charmer
- ☐10. Vipero the Snake Man
- ☐11. Arachnid the King of Spiders
- ☐12. Trillion the Three-Headed Lion

Beast Quest:
The Dark Realm

- ☐13. Torgor the Minotaur
- ☐14. Skor the Winged Stallion
- ☐15. Narga the Sea Monster
- ☐16. Kaymon the Gorgon Hound
- ☐17. Tusk the Mighty Mammoth
- ☐18. Sting the Scorpion Man

Beast Quest:
The Amulet of Avantia

- ☐19. Nixa the Death Bringer
- ☐20. Equinus the Spirit Horse
- ☐21. Rashouk the Cave Troll
- ☐22. Luna the Moon Wolf
- ☐23. Blaze the Ice Dragon
- ☐24. Stealth the Ghost Panther

Beast Quest:
The Shade of Death

- ☐25. Krabb Master of the Sea
- ☐26. Hawkite Arrow of the Air
- ☐27. Rokk the Walking Mountain
- ☐28. Koldo the Arctic Warrior
- ☐29. Trema the Earth Lord
- ☐30. Amictus the Bug Queen

Beast Quest:
The World of Chaos

- ☐31. Komodo the Lizard King
- ☐32. Muro the Rat Monster
- ☐33. Fang the Bat Fiend
- ☐34. Murk the Swamp Man
- ☐35. Terra Curse of the Forest
- ☐36. Vespick the Wasp Queen

Beast Quest:
The Lost World

- ☐37. Convol the Cold-Blooded Brute
- ☐38. Hellion the Firey Foe
- ☐39. Krestor the Crushing Terror
- ☐40. Madara the Midnight Warrior
- ☐41. Ellik the Lightning Horror
- ☐42. Carnivora the Winged Scavenger

Beast Quest:
The Pirate King

- ☐43. Balisk the Water Snake
- ☐44. Koron Jaws of Death
- ☐45. Hecton the Body Snatcher
- ☐46. Torno the Hurricane Dragon
- ☐47. Kronos the Clawed Menace
- ☐48. Bloodboar the Buried Doom

Special Bumper Editions

- ☐Vedra & Krimon: Twin Beasts of Avantia
- ☐Spiros the Ghost Phoenix
- ☐Arax the Soul Stealer
- ☐Kragos & Kildor: The Two-Headed Demon
- ☐Creta the Winged Terror
- ☐Mortaxe the Skeleton Warrior
- ☐Ravira Ruler of the Underworld
- ☐Raksha the Mirror Demon

All books priced at £4.99,
special bumper editions
priced at £5.99.

Series 6

BEAST QUEST

Can Tom and his companions rescue his mother from the clutches of evil Velmal...?

978 1 40830 723 6

978 1 40830 724 3

978 1 40830 725 0

978 1 40830 726 7

978 1 40830 727 4

978 1 40830 728 1

978 1 40830 735 9

Does Tom have the strength to triumph over cunning Creta?

Series 7: THE LOST WORLD

OUT NOW!

978 1 40830 729 8

978 1 40830 730 4

978 1 40830 731 1

978 1 40830 732 8

978 1 40830 733 5

978 1 40830 734 2